2.0   0.5pts

D1402807

Don't Cry, Lion!

Dandi Daley Mackall

ILLUSTRATED BY

Elena Kucharik

Tommy
NELSON
www.tommynelson.com
A Division of Thomas Nelson, Inc.
www.ThomasNelson.com

Published in Nashville, Tennessee, by Tommy Nelson™,
a division of Thomas Nelson, Inc.

Library of Congress Cataloging-in-Publication Data

Mackall, Dandi Daley.
     Don't cry, lion! / Dandi Daley Mackall; illustrated by Elena Kucharik.
        p. cm. – (I'm not afraid)
     Summary: When he is thrown into a pit with a big, mean lion, a little lion is
frightened until Daniel shows him that God is bigger than any bully.
     ISBN 0-8499-7753-3
     [1. Lions—Fiction. 2. Bullies—Fiction. 3. Prayer—Fiction. 4. Daniel (Biblical
character)—Fiction. 5. Stories in rhyme.] I. Kucharik, Elena ill. II Title.

PZ8.3.M179 Do 2001
[E]—dc21

                                                          2001042762

Printed in Singapore
01 02 03 04 05 TWP 5 4 3 2 1

I used to know the king of mean.
His roar could stop a crowd.
They called him Big-Mouth Leo,
And I ran when he got loud.

Then one day I was captured, caged,
And thrown into a pit—
With lions, lions everywhere,
And not a place to sit!

Angry lions growled and fought
And snarled as I walked by.
With no way out, I heard a shout,
"Hey! Get the little guy!"

I hurried off and tried to find
A safer place to hide.
Instead I turned, and just my luck . . .
"Big Leo? No!" I cried.

"This den is mine!" that big mouth roared.
"And you'll do what I say!
'Cause I'm the meanest, keenest king,
Who always gets his way!"

"Come on—I'm just a scaredy-cat!"
I tried to back away.
"Don't bully me," I begged of him.
And then I thought to pray.

That very moment up above
A hand drew back the gates.
"We told you, Daniel, not to pray!"
"The lion's den awaits!"

Then down, down, down came Daniel,
Heading straight for Leo's claws!
"You're just in time for dinner!"
Leo opened wide his jaws.

Then suddenly, an angel came!
"Now don't behave this way!
You're much too bossy, Leo.
Daniel showed you how to pray."

And all at once he saw the light.
That lion understood!
He shut his big mouth very tight
And promised to be good.

I thanked the angel—Daniel too.
Then Daniel gave a nod:
"That bully might be pretty big,
   But not as big as God!"

So when you meet a bully,
Who is twice as big as you,
You've heard it from the lion's mouth:
Ask God to help you, too!